Printed in the European Union on environmentally friendly, chlorine- and acid-free paper.

www.united-pc.eu

BEGOTTEN OBSERVATIONS

BY ZAIDA BHIKA

PREFACE

The exposition that follows

On experiences vital

Is of function that allows

For differences actual

And also a correlation that bellows

For conferences casual

With a communication that fellows

References loyal.

CONTENTS

21. Promise
22. Deliverance
23. Frustration
24. Equality
25. Revolution
26. Emotion
27. Faith
28. Cheer
29. Opinion
30. Hope
31. Failing Courage
32. Courage
33. Intrigue
34. Beauty
35. Circumstance
36. Departure
37. Enticement
38. Fallacy
39. Honesty
40. Desire

41. Pride
42. Approval
43. Foolery
44. Integrity
45 Luck
46. Advice
47. Allegiance
48. Vocation
49. Challenge
50. Comedy
51. Determination
52. Doubt
53. Enthusiasm
54. Humdrum
55. Indecision
56. Mockery
57. Motive
58. Pandemonium
59. Pity
60. Practice

61. Problem
62. The Unexpected
63. Power
64. Regret
65. Habit
66. Excitement
67. Fortune
68. Morality
69. Chance
70. Obligation
71. Predicament
72. Preparations
73. Fact
74. Guarantee
75. Surprise
76. Precautions
77. Sorrows
78. Compromise
79. Conspiracy
80. Consideration

1. <u>Invention</u>

Necessity provokes remedy
Introducing hope to an extremity
And delivering periphery
From untold calamity,
That opens destiny
To an unparalleled itinerary
Uplifting all within proximity.

2. <u>Justice</u>

In order to exercise what is righteous
One must abandon, of malicious
And all that is suspicious;
As well as, treacherous.
Then to secure the efficacious
By way of courteous –
And acts virtuous;
Lending to the prosperous.

3. Adrift

When things appear aimless
Or completely purposeless –
Minus goal, direction and so pointless,
Enters lethargy, together with careless,
That maintains a faltering, reckless,
And so , perpetuating routes choiceless.

4. Reconciliation

The setting of an agreement
That conveys an adjustment
For an appeasement,
Is a working arrangement
That initiates improvement,
From disharmony to attunement
And is further conducive to enlightenment.

5. <u>Influence</u>

When significance
Carries pressure or predominance
And controls importance,
The impact has ascendance
That credits countenance,
With a domination and governance,
Prompting a remembrance
And then, seducing performance.

6. <u>Protection</u>

Sheltered from all cold
Protected from many a storm
Guarded so, from tempest
Re-enforced from bitter
Secured from unwarmed
Bound away from frozen
Defended from chill
Strengthened from iciness.

7. Options

When presented with distinctions
The opportunity opens for discretions,
Preferences and evaluations,
That are of benefit for commissions.
The advantage being of augmentations,
The privilege lies in determinations,
Hence, on matters of choice, expansions.

8. Acceptance

The admittance of facts
Together with a recognition, enacts
A confirmation that contacts,
An embracement of extracts.
This maintenance impacts,
And is of obedient abstracts.

9. <u>Despondent</u>

Ambitions no longer materialize
Despite efforts to revitalize;
Then hope accepts
Without precepts;
As indifference settles
And with nettles.

10. <u>Ideality</u>

If all would share
With a sense of aware
Despite wear
Or fears of bare;
Initiate care
And with dare,
Then this flair
Would hold, for all things fair.

11. <u>Freedom</u>

Consign the uplifting
Of all constraint,
And then resign to the drifting
Of all complaint
But with design of sifting
Of all plaint.

12. <u>Ousting</u>

What is fair and just
Demands a stand –
But the right and must
Requires a hand –
To implement the new and bust
Of the forgone brand.
Then the change and to adjust
Carries grand
Summoning for courage and trust -
The play of a new band.

13. Values

Embedded in doctrine
And rooted in discipline
Lies outline,
That promotes superfine
As a means to the divine.

14. Confusion

All of fluster and in a state of befuddlement
Agitated and to a point of bewilderment
Perplexed, till there is embarrassment.
This apparent bother or derangement
Disregards, and hence this bafflement
Ends but in further entanglement,
That then overthrows fundament.

15. Plight

When faced with a difficulty
That unfolds a perplexity,
In its extremity –
Trouble and calamity,
Are fact, embracing eventuality.
The impediment in complexity
Is inhibiting and filled with timidity –
In short, a position for warranty.

16. Remedy

Assistance that caters
For hurt, and barters
Is a mend that alters -
From ruin and tatters
To a redress that matters.
This conciliate includes chatters
That are of excitable raters,
Until, participant masters.

17. Pleasure

With relaxation the demand
Recreation lends a hand
Then diversion in reprimand
Meets jollification, super-grand.
And as celebration makes a stand
With titillation the just command
Satisfaction is granted, well inland
With gratification, holding band.
Hence, facilitation acting as errand.

18. Bustle

With much ado and flurry
In times of hubbub and hurry
When fuss begins to curry,
Tumult signals carry
And dash is the only worry.
Here hassle is of parry
And play is all of scurry;
The unsettledness, but of larry.

19. Trauma

Imprisoned in confusion
And obscure of direction
Debased in valuation
And insecure of proposition
Weathered in incomprehension
And, even unsure of consolation
Depressed in a demoralization
And demur in connotation.

20. Awaiting

Expectancies paint
Blatancies of plaint
Till emergencies faint
Equate to fantasies that ain't.

21. Promise

The taking on of a commitment
That guarantees, as well as, is of agreement
Is a preoccupation or presentiment
Of a declaration and engagement,
That secures compromise in the arrangement
And settles for an endorsement,
Contracting a bond with inducement
And coaxing expectation through enticement.

22. Deliverance

Lifted from a depth
That has drowned
Then sifted of worth
That has owned
Then rifted from dearth
That has bound
At last, uplifted from wrath
That has wound.

23. <u>Frustration</u>

Gripped by closure
And ripped of assure
Stands tipped a venture
That is stripped of measure.

24. <u>Equality</u>

The advocate for alikeness
That is based on identicalness
And carries a oneness
Is based on much shapeliness;
But the selfsameness
Does not account for the variedness
In the absoluteness
Of fairness.

25. <u>Revolution</u>

Insinuating favour and ingratiating amour
Inviting candour and intimating splendour
Inciting succor and insisting saviour
Inaugurating honour and instigating flavour
Instituting clamour and incorporating dour
Inculcating devour and indicating hour
Inserting vigour and incapacitating rancour
This is an investigating of parlour and initiating
of demeanour.

26. <u>Emotion</u>

Of belief and motive
They ration and contrive
Upon the introspective
Carrying appreciation and drive.
With a need for educating, in order to survive
They must, at that, be subjective,
In judgments of value that derive,
And hold out for a discipline to thrive,
Amid experience, so avoiding all repressive.

27. Faith

Elements of certainty
Connoting integrity
And based on psychological complexity,
Require, hence, a context of mentality
As well as audacity
And hold for will, activity.
They are an act of total personality
Involving freedom as substantiality
And finally, demand surrender to priority
From all things comprising gravity.

28. Cheer

Optimism filled with jubilation
Delights with animation
Celebrating acclamation,
That then activates ovation.
The applause holds approbation
Rooted in laudation
And diverts in its salutation.
The tickle is of gratification
And rests in alleviation.

29. <u>Opinion</u>

To pass judgment
Or compliment
Minus all argument
Even experiment
And still evoke inducement,
Is a consequence of attunement,
Held sentiment,
Meaningful acknowledgement
And active intendment.

30. <u>Hope</u>

Expectation marked with confidence
Immersed in credence
And vehemence,
For future reward and conscience,
Is a source of timeless existence
That anticipates a favourable incidence
Under Our Maker's excellence.

31. <u>Failing Courage</u>

When there is uncertainness
Pain, hardship or nervousness
And acts entail a recklessness,
With further, irresolution, timidity and wariness
Patience, tolerance and carefulness
Are lacking in fearlessness.

32. <u>Courage</u>

Morally, the ability to act rightly, with
sufferance
Requires a willingness and perseverance
In choices made with affirmance
So, that obstacles that obscure a forbearance
Are removed, and there is endurance
In their confrontation with tolerance.

33. Intrigue

Secrecy captivates
Till discreet planning fascinates
With a hidden plot that animates,
And an enigma sensational that postulates,
Then curiosity invigorates
And a stupefaction invigilates.

34. Beauty

This perpetual experience carries excitation
It is a governing of our feelings of attraction
Affording both pleasure and satisfaction –
And lending to a source of gratification.
Hence, when in the process of admiration
It holds for features of absolute perfection,
And those balanced and harmonious in
composition.

35. Circumstance

Drawn out facts
Relevant to acts
That respect pacts
And of times enacts.
Whatever, the case contracts;
Whether doom reacts
Or some other event compacts;
Detail, alone, contracts,
As concern distracts.

36. Departure

When there is a deviation from expected
An abandonment from respected
The withdrawal is directed
To an adieu injected
From an escape infected.
This embarkation ejected
Truly is a desertion erected.

37. <u>Enticement</u>

A trap set with allurement
One, of a call about seducement -
Here, an invitation with encouragement
Or appeal full of enchantment -
Is of persuasion serving as an inducement,
An influence as in an entrapment,
And goading and baiting, beside predicament.

38. <u>Fallacy</u>

Whether intentional or unintentional
In the desire, to manipulate or simply on the play
conversational,
How is it that arguments, unsound, and also illogical
Deceive, delude and even elude to calculations vital?
In the case of disbeliefs and truths not proven - natural;
But nonetheless, faulty reasoning does convey the irratio
With apprehension and misjudgment the only final.

39. Honesty

When straightforwardness
Together with a directness
Indicate an uprightness,
Sincerity and honourableness,
Hold for righteousness.
But such openness,
That carries a bluntness,
Shows, however, artlessness,
In terms of the outspokenness.

40. Desire

When longing and wanting
Excite with a planting
Action is taken, that then in jaunting
Wills and motivates, hence granting,
Fundamentally, pleasure, that is enchanting.
But if impeded by conventions slanting
Or postponed by a higher chanting
Then hopes are thwarted from no flaunting,
And dreams embittered with much ranting.

41. Pride

Self-esteem or egoism
That carries self-respect and egotism
Is filled with self-confidence and narcissism,
Self-importance and dynamism.
The self-regard or ego-centrism
Is of self-interest with exhibitionism
And hence a self-administration leaning
towards amoralism.

42. Approval

When granted the consent
For a deed acceptable ,
The support in assent
Is so inseparable
From a go-ahead with intent
To a compliance immeasurable
That license patent
Validates, further action recommendable.

43. Foolery

Behaviour immersed in irrationality
That carries every inch of irresponsibility
Is in every way an unpracticality,
Denotes, at that insensibility
And is nothing but an absurdity,
That is as preposterous as extremity.

44. Integrity

Being honest in principle and holding for incorruptibility
Is a quality of truthfulness and authenticity,
That requires a consistency and veracity,
In virtues and actions, together with a responsibility.
Here also, with these adjustments, an accountability,
The accuracy of the doing embracing a flexibility.

45. <u>Luck</u>

Of a godsend bearing an advantage
Prosperity shifts bringing leverage,
With happiness on board as heritage.
Both occasion and manage,
Are of an opportunity with bondage,
As break offers patronage
And blessing, but equating to encourage.

46. <u>Advice</u>

When for premature action
There is a recommendation
The very consultation
Is filled with such instruction
That the information
Serves as a prescription
Or suggestion
Either for a two-fold reflection
Or farewell correction.

47. <u>Allegiance</u>

Commitment with a loyalty
That is filled with fealty
Carries a fidelity
That sustains piety.
Its tenacity
Is based on servility,
That carries duty
With a vivacity,
But to a point of docility.
This devotion in its sanctity
Functions as in charity.

48. <u>Vocation</u>

When strong feelings exist for one's occupation
Together with the use of one's gifts in the commission
And there is evidence of a dedication,
The employment grants much gratification,
So too, if there is reconciliation,
Between the exertion and qualification;
In being drawn to the profession,
Respectability is set with an obligation.

49. <u>Challenge</u>

When called to participate in a situation
competitive
Importance lies in being objective,
On the one hand, entertaining matters restive
And on the other, allowing for the speculative.
This provocation can be exhaustive
But initiates for ultimatums curative.

50. <u>Comedy</u>

Entertainment capricious
That provokes of the delirious
Is often ludicrous
If not ridiculous.
But it can also be facetious
Or there again, hilarious.
These shocks all joyous
Are momentous,
Of conventions, fabulous.

51. <u>Determination</u>

A dedication towards one's business
Together with purpose that carries firmness
Requires conviction and steadfastness,
In calculations, establishing a boldness,
That will demand a dauntlessness,
And that serves together with a doggedness.
In fine, the resolve, should of craftiness
Better, in both mastery and cleverness.

52. <u>Doubt</u>

In difficulty
Or with ambiguity
Where there is uncertainty,
Appears incredulity
That off-sets anxiety,
Together with misgiving and irregularity,
And distrust and implausibility.
This suspense of dubiety
Makes for an impassibility
Problems with sensibility.

53. Enthusiasm

Associated with merriment
Even holding for excitement
This ardour carries an enjoyment
That exhilarates with enactment,
Inducing a fever with enchantment
Filled with energy and ferment.
The devotion vehement,
Spirited and warm, in sentiment
Is a dash in avouchment.

54. Humdrum

Monotonous routine or the everyday
That is lacking in excitement and gay
Is a plodding, every inch of the way
That has, commonplace as the only say.
This drab uninteresting, offers nay,
Is a tedious and pedestrian play -
With the ordinary, resulting in delay.

55. Indecision

Uncertainty provokes
Causing hesitation that evokes
Till indecisiveness chokes
And doubt pokes.
This results in irresolution which yokes
Until, vacillation ends jokes.

56. Mockery

Jokes contemptuous
That tease with the unchivalrous
Are injurious
As the sham is presumptuous –
A butt audacious,
And farce discourteous.
The travesty is, in short, venomous.

57. <u>Motive</u>

The impulse and drive
For doing something and thrive
Is an idea conceived, and of contrive;
And that is based on a rationale with strive.
Here the grounds or basis revive,
All whilst, passions derive;
Its very influence, bearing survive.

58. <u>Pandemonium</u>

In chaos and clatter
Commotions do not cease to matter
And confusion, together with natter,
Carries clamour, including all ranter.
Craziness is the chatter –
Indeed, contrariety holds this prater.

59. Pity

When a condolence
However of benevolence
Carries ebullience
And indulgence,
The sympathy in beneficence
Although of reference
Eludes, to feelings of impotence
As the comfort admits innocence.

60. Practice

With constant repetition
And emphasized imitation
Arises, moments of disillusion,
And oft hours of procrastination.
This action, however, on completion
Solves in matters of inhibition.

61. Problem

With difficulties arise questions
That pose headaches and botherations.
These troubles that carry complications
Cause obstacles in situations
Because ideas are based in successions.
Here, dilemmas therefore, the conclusions.

62. The Unexpected

Happening unforeseen
That carries startling and obscene
Is of chance that is seen,
And accident not preen.
The surprise is keen
And an eye-opening full of demean,
And, that suddenly, breaks from routine.

63. <u>Power</u>

A control that has influence,
Functions with competence,
And has convenience,
Is dynamic in prevalence,
As execution has concurrence
On potentialities and intelligence,
That afford prominence.
This zest carries insistence,
That as associated with indulgence,
Shows in its willingness for complacence.

64. <u>Regret</u>

Upset over past action
Carries heartache and contrition
Of qualms and dissatisfaction
That bemoan with mortification
And mourn in exasperation.
This hopelessness or indisposition
Is pain carrying lamentation
Of brood and dejection
And a bewail of compunction.

65. Habit

Of fixed attitude or constitution
Manner sets to a gravitation
And then to a mode of inclination.
So fashioned by this predisposition
The setting remains of impulsion
With make-up, of bent estimation.

66. Excitement

Amid much fuss and commotion
Activity holds for emotion
That in act, carries provocation
A bothering, of animation
And dash to an instigation.
The frenzy leads to an intoxication;
Thrill and tumult, amounting to perturbation.

67. <u>Fortune</u>

Of abundance with ampleness
Luck wins prosperousness
That fate in its wealthiness
Cannot chance, with such successfulness.
The good in its plenteousness
Has resource in inventiveness,
Course in resourcefulness
And the means to happiness.

68. <u>Morality</u>

Decency moves seemliness
Till integrity and worthiness
Fashion ideals with a nobleness,
That equates to a philosophy in humanness.
The standards retain an obligingness
Which regard, kindheartedness
And merit in righteousness.

69. <u>Chance</u>

Although accidental
And even unintentional
The unforeseeable is casual,
Playing against the optional
And weighing out the eventual.

70. <u>Obligation</u>

Conscience calls for accountableness
A contract of faithfulness
That must in terms of indebtedness
Effect a persuasiveness
And point to a responsiveness.
The bond itself in its forcefulness
Is an investment in appreciativeness
And acknowledgement of thankfulness.

71. Predicament

Crisis and emergency, culminating asperity,
Also carries urgency, representing a difficulty.
This event or charge introduces, however, probability
And is a happening or likelihood of eventuality.
It is further, a checkmate in perplexity –
In short, an aggravation, in extremity.

72. Preparations

Amid commotion, lies expediency
Heralding all that is emergency
Then, order holding impotency,
Issues reason with a dominancy,
That measures agreement with accuracy
And seeks precautions with constancy.
Then as excitement sets consistency
Challenge takes on relevancy.

73. Fact

Case and even experience
That achieve permanence
And feature intelligence,
Point evidence
And detail occurrence;
Are a testimony of coincidence
And basis of essence.

74. Guarantee

Of contract or warranty,
A bond of security,
The bestowal carries certainty
Vouching surety,
And, with the charge, responsibility.
Hence, of a treaty
But here with indemnity,
One assuring immunity
And affirming authority.

75. Surprise

When marvel with revelation
Result in unexpected consternation
And curiosity and precipitation,
Then wonder and stupefaction
Strike a miscalculation
Exposing disorientation,
And overwhelming disorganization.

76. Precautions

Steps that quantify,
Measures that signify,
Present restraints that magnify
As avoidance meets rectify.
The restrictions to qualify
Seek surveillance, with defy,
Together with provisions that intensify.

77. Sorrows

Impositions adverse
Together with difficulties perverse
Contribute to suffering diverse
That lead to dejections inverse
And worries in rehearse,
Causing wretchedness and averse –
And ending In dullness, with no reverse.

78. Compromise

Bargaining executes
As agreement prosecutes
And limit constitutes.
Provision institutes
And requirement computes,
Then compact refutes
With arrangement that salutes.

79. Conspiracy

Of concealment and discretion
With plot and mystification
Plans and discriminations,
Make up for a remedy of propositions.
Tactics embrace discretion
And project is filled with invention,
Leaving sketch all but open to suggestion.

80. Consideration

Prime weightiness
Of paramount kindliness
Unfolds thoughtfulness
That of both seriousness
And obligingness
Make for agreeableness.